Secret PRINCESSES

Prize Pony

ROSIE BANKS

Wishing Star Palace

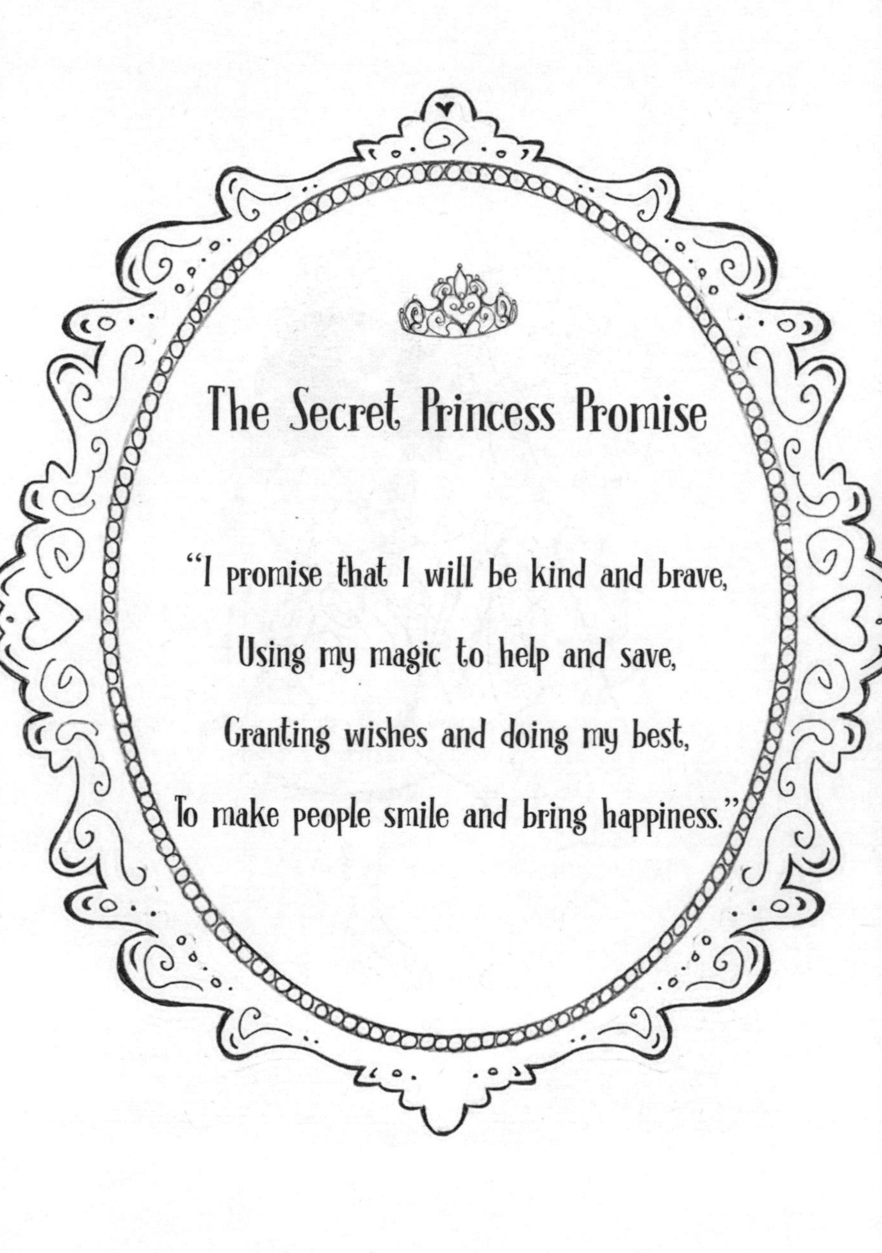

The Secret Princess Promise

"I promise that I will be kind and brave,
Using my magic to help and save,
Granting wishes and doing my best,
To make people smile and bring happiness."

CONTENTS

CHAPTER ONE
A Mysterious Arrival

"Does this look OK, Gran?" Mia held up the toy mouse she was making for her cat, Flossie. It was made out of white felt with a pink ribbon for a tail.

Her grandma put down her knitting. She was looking after Mia for the day. Mia loved it when it was just her and Gran because they always did fun craft projects.

"It's great," Gran said. "Now you just need the secret ingredient."

"What secret ingredient?" Mia asked curiously.

Gran took a plastic container out of her tapestry bag. "Catnip!" she said. "Cats really love catnip."

Gran showed Mia how to fill the mouse with the dried herbs, and then Mia began the final bit of sewing. As she leant over with her needle, the golden pendant she was wearing fell forward. It was shaped like half a heart and it had a ruby embedded in it. The ruby glittered in the sunlight streaming in through the window.

"Your necklace is very pretty," said Gran.

"Is it new?" she asked.

"I've had it a few months now – I got it when Charlotte went to live in America," said Mia. "She has a matching one. We wear them all the time."

Gran smiled. "To help you remember each other? That's lovely."

"Mmm," said Mia, wondering what Gran would say if she told her the truth – that she didn't need a necklace to remember Charlotte, because she and Charlotte still saw each other all the time. Their necklaces were magic! Whenever their pendants started to glow, the girls were whisked away to an enchanted palace in the clouds.

Mia remembered how astonished she and Charlotte had been when they'd first visited Wishing Star Palace. It had been like having an amazing dream together – particularly when they discovered that they had been chosen to train to be Secret Princesses. Secret Princesses could grant wishes to make people happy. They all lived in the real world, but they met up at Wishing Star Palace to have lots of magical, princessy fun. Every time Mia and Charlotte had visited the palace they had gone on an adventure and helped someone by using magic.

I really hope we go back to the palace soon, thought Mia as she finished her toy mouse. She jumped to her feet. "Here, kitty!" she called. "Flossie!"

Flossie came trotting through from the kitchen.

Kneeling down, Mia made the toy scurry along the ground like a real mouse. Flossie's green eyes widened and she pounced. Mia let go just in time as Flossie grabbed the

mouse and started rolling over with it, batting it with her paws in delight.

Gran smiled. "A definite success! Cup of tea time, I think. Would you like a hot chocolate?"

"Yes, please," said Mia.

Gran went into the kitchen, leaving Mia to carry on playing with Flossie. As Flossie rolled and pounced, Mia was reminded of Baxter, the bouncy puppy she and Charlotte had met on their last Secret Princess adventure. His owner, Tessa, had wished that he would pass a test at puppy-training school so that he could go on holiday with her. Mia and Charlotte had helped her train Baxter and, at the end of their adventure, a glittering ruby had appeared in each of their pendants. If they granted three more wishes and collected three more rubies, they would pass their second stage of training and get beautiful magic slippers to wear whenever they were at Wishing Star Palace.

A flash of light suddenly sparked across the surface of the pendant. Mia caught her breath as the whole pendant started to sparkle brightly. It was time for another magical adventure!

She glanced quickly at the door, but Gran was still in the kitchen making their drinks. Luckily, no time would pass at home while she was away on a Secret Princess adventure, so Gran wouldn't even notice that she was gone.

Mia wrapped her hand around the pendant and felt tingles running through her fingers. "I wish I could see Charlotte again," she whispered excitedly.

Light streamed out of the pendant and

surrounded her in a glowing whirlwind of sparkles. Giving a squeal of delight, Mia felt herself being whisked away.

She twirled round and round like a ballerina until finally her feet landed on solid ground. The light cleared. Mia blinked, expecting to see the gardens of Wishing Star Palace, but she discovered she was standing in the middle of a sunny meadow at the foot of a hill. Scarlet poppies and golden buttercups danced in the breeze and pretty blue butterflies were swooping through the air. In the distance, Mia could see the pointed turrets of Wishing Star Palace reaching up into the blue sky.

It was beautiful, but Mia felt confused.

Why was she so far away from the palace? Had the magic somehow gone wrong? She looked down and saw that she was wearing her golden princess dress and when she put her hand to her blonde hair, she felt her tiara nestling there.

"Mia!"

Charlotte appeared in the meadow in her rose-pink princess dress and a glittering diamond tiara. Her brown curls bounced on her shoulders and her hazel eyes sparkled with excitement. She raced towards Mia and swung her round in a tight hug. "Oh, it's so good to see you again!"

"And you! But where are we?" said Mia, hugging her back.

Charlotte looked round and Mia saw her frown as she realised they weren't in the gardens of the palace. "Weird. Do you think the magic's gone wrong?"

"That's what I was thinking," said Mia.

"I wonder where the princesses are."

Charlotte put her hands to her mouth and shouted. "Hello! Is anyone there?"

All they heard was the gentle rustling of the grass and flowers in reply.

Charlotte gave Mia a confused look. "It's a mystery! Maybe we should just start walking to the palace." She held out her hand. Mia was about to take it when they heard an echoey voice.

"Hellooooooo!"

They looked round.

"Hellooooooo!" The voice came again. "In heeeeeeeeere!"

"I think it's coming from *inside* the hill," said Charlotte in surprise. "Come on! Let's go and investigate!"

"Wait!" Mia grabbed her. "What if it's Princess Poison?"

Princess Poison was a Secret Princess who had turned bad and used her magic to ruin people's wishes. Every time she managed to make someone unhappy, she became more powerful. So far, she had turned up on every one of Charlotte and Mia's adventures – but, by working together, they had always managed to beat her!

"Come and seeeeeeeeeee!" said the voice.

Charlotte frowned. "It can't be Princess Poison because she's been banished from Wishing Star Palace. Let's try and find whoever it is."

Holding hands, they walked cautiously towards the hill.

"In heeeeeeeeeeeeeere!"

Charlotte pointed to a dark opening in the base of the hill. "There's a cave! The voice is coming from in there!"

Heart pounding, Mia followed her best friend to the cave entrance. It looked dark and gloomy.

Whatever were they going to find inside?

The girls edged into the cave. "Hello?" Charlotte called. "Who's in here?"

"Me! Come in deeper!"

"It sounds like Princess Ella," Mia said.

Last time the girls had come to Wishing Star Palace, Princess Poison's horrible parrot, Venom, had stolen Princess Ella's wand. If Princess Poison managed to spoil someone's wish using Ella's wand, poor Ella would be banished from Wishing Star Palace for ever.

The girls had vowed to do everything they could to stop that from happening and to get Ella's wand back.

Mia and Charlotte went further into the cave and round a bend in the rock. Then they both stopped and gasped. There were strings of twinkly lights all around the walls and in the centre of the cavern lay a large purple creature. She was curled up asleep, her head resting on her front feet and her ridged tail curled around her, reminding Mia of how her cat, Flossie, sometimes slept. Her amethyst scales glittered in the light.

"Oh my goodness!" squeaked Charlotte. "It's a dragon!"

CHAPTER TWO

A Dragon Birthday

Mia stared at the beautiful creature in front of them. The dragon opened her eyes. They were a deep, dark purple.

"Don't worry, she's very gentle," said Princess Ella, appearing from the back of the cavern. She waved at the girls and, lifting up the skirts of her long blue dress, she climbed carefully over the dragon's legs.

She had short dark hair and almond-shaped eyes and there was a paw print pendant on her necklace. Each princess's pendant reflected her own special talent. Mia and Charlotte had half hearts because they were training to become Friendship Princesses, who always worked as a team.

"I'm so glad you're here," Princess Ella said, hurrying over to them. "I was really hoping the magic would bring you in time."

"But … it's a dragon …" stammered Charlotte, pointing.

"Yes. Shh!" Princess Ella put her fingers to her lips. "She's resting. She's had a long flight to get here. Dragons don't live in the Wishing Star Palace grounds, they just

come for special occasions."

"Why, what's happening?" said Mia.

The dragon gently moved her tail and the girls saw two large lilac eggs cradled against her body.

"She came so her babies can hatch out in this cave," Princess Ella explained. "It's really rare to see a baby dragon hatch. It only happens about once a century."

"Oh, wow!" whispered Mia.

The mother dragon lifted her head and breathed out. Purple flames shot out of her nostrils and surrounded her eggs. Charlotte gasped and even Mia shrank back, but Princess Ella smiled. "It's OK. Her flames can't hurt you!"

Mia realised that the flames were made of glittering sparks of purple light. Small cracks suddenly started to appear in the surface of the eggs.

"It's happening!" breathed Ella. "The babies are about to hatch!"

Mia and Charlotte watched in awe as the cracks ran over the eggs. There was a tapping noise and suddenly the top of each egg broke off. Two dragon babies wriggled and started to clamber out of the eggs.

One of them had soft rose-pink scales. The other dragon was a bit smaller and had baby blue scales.

The mother dragon breathed another stream of glittering purple flames on them. As the light covered the dragons, the baby dragons lifted their heads.

"GRWWWK!" croaked the pink dragon, nudging the blue one playfully.

He rolled over on to his back and the pink dragon pounced on him. They tumbled over and over like two giant kittens.

"They're adorable!" said Mia.

As she spoke, the babies seemed to notice her for the first time. They stopped playing and approached the girls and Princess Ella. The blue dragon was more timid and hid behind his sister. The pink dragon stopped by Mia, who held out her hand.

"GRWWWK!" the pink dragon said and she rubbed the side of her face against Mia's fingers. Her scales were smooth and shiny. Mia scratched the dragon under her chin

and it made a noise like Flossie purring – but much louder! Then it stretched its tiny wings out and flapped them. Mia giggled and the dragon looked surprised.

The blue dragon sidled up to Charlotte and cautiously offered her a paw. When she took it, the dragon rolled over on his back. She crouched down and tickled his tummy. He made delighted squeaking noises. "You're the cutest thing I've ever seen!" Charlotte told him.

Mia turned to Ella, her eyes shining. "I'm so glad we got here in time to see them being born."

Princess Ella smiled at her. "We should think of some nice names for the babies.

Have you got any ideas?"

The girls looked at the baby dragons. Mia tried a few names out in her head – Sparkle and Glitter, Lilac and Bluebell, Sugar and Spice. But none of them seemed quite right.

"I can't think of anything," said Charlotte, shaking her head.

"Well, we can give it some more thought back at the palace," said Ella. "We should leave the mother and her babies in peace now. I know all the other princesses will want to see you. And Princess Sylvie is baking a special chocolate dragon cake."

"Yum!" said Charlotte. Princess Sylvie made the most delicious cakes ever!

Ella kissed the mother dragon goodbye and the girls gave the babies a last cuddle, then they all made their way back to the meadow.

"I don't have my wand, so I'll use my princess shoes to get back to the palace. Hold my hands and the magic will take us there," said Princess Ella.

"You'll get your wand back soon," said Charlotte reassuringly.

Ella smiled sadly. "I miss it so much. I hate the thought that if Princess Poison uses it to spoil a wish I might never see the amazing animals at Wishing Star Palace again."

"We won't let that happen," Mia promised her.

"Thank you so much, girls," said Ella, squeezing their hands. "If you keep granting wishes, you'll soon pass the second stage of training and get your own slippers to wear."

Mia crossed her fingers. She really hoped that happened soon!

Princess Ella tapped her heels together. "To the palace!" she cried.

Over the meadow they spun, past the pond where flamingo-like birds were

splashing in the sun. They flew past huge bouncy trampolines and a carousel with carved wooden animals to ride, and over the palace's gardens where bright flowers blossomed everywhere and the trees had candyfloss hanging from their branches.

The magic set them down in a large living room. Sun streamed in through the windows and garlands of sweet-smelling flowers decorated the room. Some princesses with pretty dresses and sparkling tiaras were sitting at a table.

Everyone jumped to their feet to say hello.

"It's so lovely to see you!" said Alice, hugging the girls. She had strawberry-blonde hair with cool red streaks in, and

she wore a deep red princess gown and a pendant shaped like a musical note. Alice had been the girls' babysitter until she had won a TV talent show and become a pop star. It was Alice who had first brought Mia and Charlotte to Wishing Star Palace and told them all about the Secret Princesses.

Turning to a short princess with straight black hair standing next to her, Alice said, "Girls, this is Princess Kiko. I don't think you've met before."

"We saw you last time we were here," Charlotte said. "Bouncing on the trampolines. You're a gymnast, right?"

"That's right," said Princess Kiko, smiling. "I hear that you do gymnastics, too."

"Charlotte's brilliant at gymnastics," said Mia, proudly.

"Did you see the dragon?" Princess Kiko asked them.

"Not just one dragon, three!" said Mia.

Princess Sophie, who had long dark hair and a paintbrush pendant, gasped. "The babies have hatched?"

"Yes, there's one boy and one girl," said Princess Ella. "You'll have to come and paint them, Sophie. We could put a picture of them up on the wall in here."

"Oh yes!" cried Princess Sophie, clasping her hands together.

"I'll have to make up a song about dragons," said Alice.

"That would be brilliant!" said Mia.

"In fact, it would be *roar*-some!" said Charlotte with a grin.

Just then a princess with deep red hair and a cupcake pendant came hurrying in with a large jug. "I thought I heard you two arrive!" Princess Sylvie said, coming in with an enormous chocolate cake shaped like an egg. "You're just in time for some of my dragon cake. Would you like some?"

"Yes, please!" Charlotte and Mia said together. Everyone gathered around the table. The cake looked delicious – like a giant Easter egg resting in a nest made of sugar leaves and flowers. Princess Sylvie pulled out her wand and tapped the cake.

Four long cracks ran down the egg and a hole appeared in the top. Purple sparkles shot out and then the cracks widened. Pieces of the shell fell apart, revealing a chocolate cake shaped exactly like a baby dragon!

Everyone clapped. Princess Sylvie curtseyed modestly and soon they were all eating slices of the most delicious chocolate fudge cake that Mia had ever tasted.

Then there were pieces of chocolate eggshell and sweet sugar flowers to eat, all washed down with fruit juice that tasted like fresh strawberries.

"This is so yummy!" Mia said, licking her fingers happily.

"I wish I could eat your chocolate cake every day, Princess Sylvie," Charlotte agreed.

Princess Sylvie looked pleased. "Oh, thank you—" She broke off with a gasp as her wand started to glow.

The other princesses looked down – their wands were all glowing too.

"Someone needs a wish granting!" exclaimed Alice.

Charlotte jumped to her feet. "Mia and I will do it!"

Mia nodded. "Definitely!"

"Oh yes! It's the perfect chance for you to earn your next rubies," said Alice.

"Be careful of Princess Poison, girls," warned Princess Sylvie anxiously. "She's sure to try and stop you."

"We don't care!" said Charlotte bravely.

Mia turned to Princess Ella, who was the only princess without a wand in her hand. "If we do see her, we'll do everything we can to stop her from spoiling a wish and get your wand back."

Grateful tears glistened in Ella's eyes.

Charlotte nodded in agreement. "We're going to grant a wish and get your wand back and no one – not Princess Poison, or her servant Hex, or any of her mean pets – will stop us!"

CHAPTER THREE

Grace

Mia and Charlotte raced up the spiral staircase towards the Mirror Room with Alice. The Magic Mirror was on a tarnished gold stand, its oval surface swirling with light. Alice touched her wand to the surface and a picture appeared in it. Mia saw a girl standing by a blue horse trailer wearing a riding hat over her light brown hair.

Her arms were around the neck of a pretty chestnut brown pony.

There was a rhyme underneath the picture. Charlotte read it out:

"A wish needs granting, adventures await,
Call Grace's name, don't hesitate!"

Mia and Charlotte knew what to do. "Grace!" they cried.

The image in the mirror vanished and light started swirling over the surface again. It got faster and faster, forming a glowing tunnel.

"Here we go!" cried Charlotte in excitement as they felt themselves being sucked into the tunnel. They whizzed down it as if they were on a giant slide until they shot out of the end and landed in a heap under a tree.

Charlotte jumped to her feet and pulled Mia up.

Looking round, Mia saw horseboxes and trailers parked in rows, people saddling up and riding round on horses, while other people hurried about with brushes and buckets of water. "We're at a horse show!" she said.

No one had noticed their sudden arrival, but Mia knew that was all part of the special Secret Princess magic. Just then a voice crackled out of a nearby loudspeaker.

"Good morning, and welcome to the Darlingdale Junior One Day Event! The dressage will be starting in half an hour."

"How do we find Grace? There are so many people here!" said Charlotte, looking round.

"Let's start by looking for a brown horse like the one in the mirror," said Mia. "Grace is bound to be near it."

They set off to look round the trailers and horseboxes. Mia was just trying to pluck up the courage to ask someone if they knew a girl called Grace, when she spotted a chestnut brown pony being groomed.

"There!" she said, pointing. "That looks like Grace's pony!"

"It *is* Grace's pony!" Mia said as they hurried closer.

"How can you tell?" Charlotte asked.

"Look!" Mia giggled. Grace, a tall girl with a long, light-brown ponytail, was standing next to it.

Just then, Grace tripped over a box of grooming tools.

Mia and Charlotte ran forward to help her pick everything up.

"Thanks," Grace said. She smiled at them, showing the braces on her teeth. "I'm feeling so nervous. I hope Peanut is less clumsy than me when he's jumping today!"

"Peanut?" echoed Charlotte.

Grace nodded. "My pony. Well, he's not

actually *my* pony," she corrected herself. "He belongs to the stables where I go riding. He's my favourite pony there. I really want my mum and dad to buy him for me ..." Her face dropped. "But they want me to get a different one."

"Why?" said Mia, going over and stroking the shaggy pony. He had a really sweet face. "He seems nice."

"He's the best," said Grace. "He's so friendly and he always tries hard for me, but Mum and Dad want me to get a more experienced horse. But I just love Peanut." Her brown eyes welled up and she buried her face in Peanut's neck. "Sorry. I don't know why I'm telling you all this. I'm just

worried about competing today. I wish Peanut could do well to prove to Mum and Dad he's the right horse for me."

Charlotte and Mia grinned at each other. Now they knew what Grace's wish was! "I'm sure it'll be fine," said Charlotte. She patted Peanut from a cautious distance. She liked ponies, but Peanut had big hooves and she didn't want him standing on her toes!

"Do you need a hand today?" offered Mia. "We'd love to help you."

"Really? That would be great," said Grace enthusiastically. "Thank you. I'm Grace, by the way."

"I'm Charlotte, and this is Mia," Charlotte said. "What would you like us to do first?"

"Would you be able to finish grooming Peanut while I get changed?" Grace asked. "He needs to look smart for the dressage – that's the first part of the competition."

"No problem at all," said Mia. They'd helped Princess Ella groom the flying horses at Wishing Star Palace, so they knew just what to do.

While Grace went into the trailer to get changed, Charlotte brushed out Peanut's tail and Mia oiled his hooves with glossy oil. "I wish I could have a pony," Mia said. "When I'm older I'm going to have lots of horses and dogs and cats."

"And guinea pigs and rabbits and mice and probably a couple of worms as pets, too!" said Charlotte with a grin.

Mia chuckled. That was the great thing about Charlotte – they knew each other so well.

When Grace came back, she was wearing smart white leggings, long black boots and a black show jacket. "It's time for me to go to the dressage arena," she said, twisting her ponytail nervously.

"What's dressage?" Charlotte asked.

"It's a test of how obedient a horse is," Grace explained. "Each competitor goes into the arena and performs the same test in front of the judge. Do you want to come with me and watch?"

Charlotte and Mia nodded and followed her and Peanut towards the dressage ring. Grace was careful to ride Peanut around the puddles and big patches of mud so he didn't get dirty.

The steward – a smart man in a tweed coat – came over to them. "Number 201?" he said to Grace. She nodded. "You'll be going next. I hope you're ready!"

Grace gulped. "I feel so nervous," she said to Charlotte and Mia.

"Don't worry! We'll be cheering you on," said Charlotte.

Mia patted Peanut. "I bet Peanut's going to be great."

As she spoke, a large black jeep with darkened windows and an open back came driving towards them through the mud.

There were two dogs in the back of the jeep, barking loudly.

Mia realised the jeep was coming dangerously close to Peanut and Grace.

"Grace! Watch out!" she said. But before Grace could move Peanut, the driver sped up! At the last minute, the jeep swerved into a huge puddle. A wave of muddy water splashed all over Peanut and Grace!

Peanut leapt forward in surprise and Grace yelled in dismay.

The jeep drove off. As it did, Mia saw a pink fluffy poodle and a big, fierce-looking dog with a squashed-in face and a spiky collar in the back. A cackle floated out through the driver's window. "Charlotte!" she gasped. "That was Princess Poison! I recognised her dog and Hex's poodle!"

"Look what she's done to Peanut and Grace!" said Charlotte.

Mud was dripping off the pony and rider. "What am I going to do?" Grace started to cry, her shoulders shaking as she sobbed. "We can't go into the dressage looking like this!" She hugged Peanut's neck and cried into his mane. "Now Mum and Dad won't see how good you can be."

"Wait!" said Mia. "We can help you."

"How?" wailed Grace.

Mia looked at Charlotte and they both pulled out their pendants. The half hearts were sparkling and shining.

"With magic!" Mia said.

CHAPTER FOUR

Dress for Success

"Magic? What do you mean?" asked Grace, wiping away her tears.

Mia and Charlotte quickly fitted their pendants together. The two halves came together to make a whole heart. Light sparkled across the surface.

"I wish that Grace and Peanut could look really smart!" said Mia.

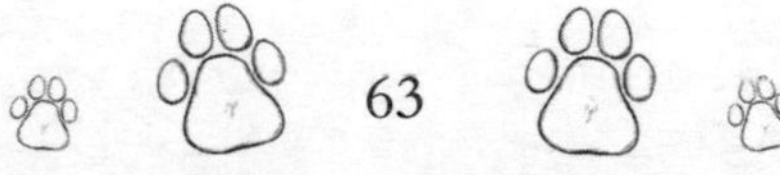

There was a flash of light and Grace gasped. "What … what just happened?"

The magic had transformed her muddy clothes into a brand-new outfit – a fitted jacket with gold buttons, spotless white gloves and white leggings. Peanut was brilliantly clean – his coat shining, his tail hanging in silky strands, his hooves shiny. There wasn't a single speck of mud on him. He looked even better than he had before!

"How did you do that?" Grace stared in astonishment.

"There's something we need to tell you," Mia whispered. "We were sent here to help you and make your wish come true."

"We can't use our magic to grant a really big wish – like making your parents buy Peanut," Charlotte put in. "But we can use it to make three smaller wishes."

"So, you used a wish to make him clean?" said Grace slowly.

They nodded.

Grace blinked and shook her head, trying to take it all in.

"Number 201!" the steward called.

"It's your turn, Grace," said Mia.

Grace still looked stunned, but didn't have time to ask them any more questions.

"Good luck!" said Charlotte. "Go and show everyone what Peanut can do."

"Oh, I hope she does well!" said Mia.

Grace rode towards the grassy arena. It had white boards around the outside and letters marking different places where Grace and Peanut had to do certain moves. Mia and Charlotte found two seats right behind the judges.

Grace rode Peanut beautifully. He did everything she asked him to, smoothly changing his pace from a walk to a trot to a canter. When Grace bowed to the judges at the end, everyone clapped loudly.

"That was the best yet," one judge said to another. "That girl's in with a chance of winning if she does well in the showjumping and cross-country rounds."

Mia really hoped he was right! She and Charlotte ran back to Grace. She was hugging Peanut. "Did you see him?" Grace asked. "He was brilliant!"

"You looked lovely," said Charlotte. "And we heard one of the judges say you've got a good chance of winning!"

"Fingers crossed," said Grace. "Will you go and see what mark I've got while I get Peanut ready for the next round?"

"Of course!" said Mia.

"I'm so glad we were able to help her," said Charlotte, as they hurried to the tent. "Princess Poison is trying to ruin things like she always does."

"Did you hear her cackle when she soaked Grace and Peanut?" said Mia.

Charlotte nodded. "She's so mean. We can't let her use Ella's wand to spoil Grace's wish, or Princess Ella won't be able to be a Secret Princess any more."

They waited anxiously as the steward filled in the scores on a big whiteboard.

As he wrote Grace's mark down Mia and Charlotte squealed. She had won!

"Let's go and tell Grace the good news!" Mia cried.

They raced across the showground, dodging dogs who were pulling their owners around on leads, swerving past people carrying buckets of water and horses with stripy rugs covering their backs to keep them warm.

A man and a woman were standing by Grace's trailer, chatting to her as she changed Peanut's saddle. "You're in the lead, Grace!" cried Mia.

Grace's face lit up. "Oh wow!" She hugged Peanut. "You clever, clever pony."

She turned to the man and woman. "Mum and Dad, this is Mia and Charlotte."

Grace's mum smiled at the girls. "Thanks for helping Grace today."

"It's no problem," said Mia. "Peanut's such a lovely pony."

"He did do surprisingly well in the dressage, didn't he?" said Grace's mum. "Considering he hasn't competed before."

"He seems like a nice pony," said her dad.

"But we'd feel better about you riding an older, more experienced horse."

Mia and Charlotte exchanged looks. Clearly Grace's parents hadn't changed their minds – yet!

Grace had changed into a shorter jacket and Peanut had white boots on his legs and a fluffy pad under his saddle. "I'm going to go and warm up for the showjumping," she told them as she swung herself up onto Peanut's saddle.

"We'll be watching from the ringside. Good luck!" her mum told her.

"Thanks!" Grace smiled and rode in the direction of the warm-up ring, with Charlotte and Mia walking beside her.

As they crossed the ground, a couple came towards them. The woman was tall and skinny, dressed in a green tweed suit. Her dark hair had an ice-white streak and she wore a hat with green feathers. The man was small and stout with mustard-yellow trousers and a brown tweed

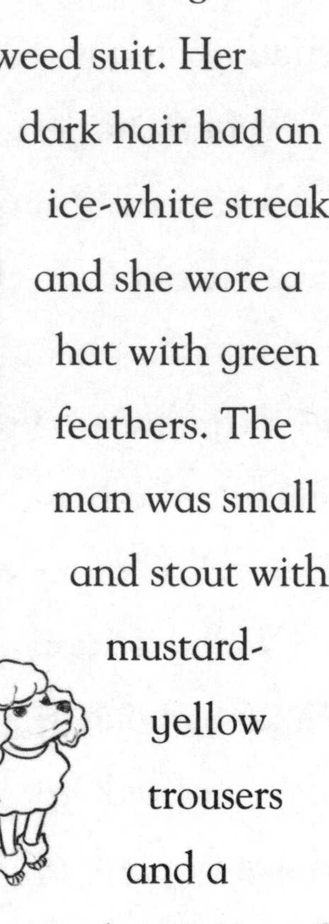

waistcoat that strained over his fat tummy. They had two dogs on leashes – a pink poodle with her nose in the air and a huge, snarling dog with a squashed face.

"Look, Charlotte," Mia whispered. "It's Princess Poison and Hex."

"And they've got Crusher and Miss Fluffy with them," groaned Charlotte.

"What are you talking about?" Grace called down from Peanut's back.

"That lady is the person who splashed you with her car," said Mia quickly.

"Well, well, well," Princess Poison drawled as she stalked over. "Who do we have here? Two goody-goodies and their new friend." She turned to Grace. "So, you want your parents to buy you that pony, do you?"

"Um, yes," Grace said cautiously.

"Well, it's not going to happen!" cackled Princess Poison.

Hex sniggered. "No! We're going to spoil your wish!"

"Oh no you won't," said Charlotte angrily. "We'll stop you!"

"Oh, really?" Princess Poison looked at

Hex and then they both dropped their dogs' leashes. Miss Fluffy and Crusher leapt towards Peanut. The big dog barked and snarled and the poodle yapped. Peanut's ears flattened and he reared up in alarm.

"Peanut!" gasped Grace, her feet falling out of the stirrups.

"Hang on, Grace!" cried Charlotte. But as Peanut leapt forward to get away from the dogs, Grace started to fall ...

CHAPTER FIVE

A Sneaky Spell

"Grace!" Mia yelled as she slipped off Peanut's back.

But just in time, Peanut put his hooves back on the ground and Grace quickly pulled herself back into the saddle.

Mia breathed a sigh of relief.

"Call your dogs off!" Charlotte shouted at Princess Poison.

"No!" Princess Poison hissed. "Get them, Crusher!"

"Frighten that pony, Miss Fluffy!" cried Hex.

Crusher snarled even more loudly and Miss Fluffy yapped shrilly. Peanut suddenly seemed to decide he had had enough. He charged straight at the dogs!

Crusher and Miss Fluffy yelped in alarm and dashed away.

"You scared them off, Peanut!" cried Grace, hugging him. "Good boy!"

"Looks like you'd better catch your pets!" Charlotte said to Princess Poison.

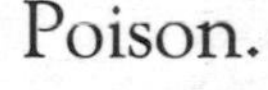

"Gah!" she spat and stomped away with Hex scuttling beside her. "This isn't over yet!" she shouted over her shoulder.

"Are you all right?" Mia asked Grace.

Grace nodded, but she looked shaken.

Mia stroked Peanut's nose and he blew gently on her hands. "You were so brave," she told him. "Most horses would have run away."

"He felt me falling and saved me," said Grace. "I can't believe that mean lady set her dogs on him."

"She's called Princess Poison," said Charlotte. "She'll do anything to stop people's wishes coming true."

"Do you think she'll try anything else today?" asked Grace anxiously.

Mia thought about Princess Poison's parting words. "Probably," she admitted.

"But don't worry, we'll stop her."

Charlotte nodded. "You just concentrate on the competition. Leave Princess Poison to us."

Grace gave them a grateful smile.

"So, how does the showjumping work?" Charlotte said.

"There are twelve jumps," Grace explained. "If your horse won't go over a jump, or if he knocks one down, you get points added to your score. The lowest score wins."

As Grace warmed Peanut up, Mia and Charlotte watched some of the other competitors go round the arena. Most of them knocked down a fence or two.

"I hope Peanut does well," said Charlotte. "If he does, Grace will stay in the lead."

Grace cantered into the ring on Peanut's back. The horse's light brown ears were pricked up and his silky tail bounced with each stride. He looked really excited about jumping.

"Come on, Grace!" breathed Mia, crossing her fingers.

There was a commotion in the seating area a bit further along from the girls. "I want a seat right at the front! Let us through!"

The girls looked round. To their dismay, they saw Princess Poison and Hex pushing their way to the front row of seats.

Grace and Peanut had started to canter round the arena, waiting for the starting bell. Grace's eyes were focused on the jumps and she hadn't noticed the commotion.

"Ladies and gentlemen, our next rider is number 201, Grace Purcell, riding Peanut!" The commentator's voice crackled over the loudspeaker.

Grace halted Peanut, bowed to the judge and then cantered towards the first jump. Peanut's ears pricked, his stride lengthened and he leapt over it, clearing the jump perfectly. He cantered on to the next jump – a white gate – and flew over that too.

"They're doing really well!" Charlotte said in delight.

Mia was watching Princess Poison. She was whispering something to Hex. "Charlotte, look!" Mia hissed in alarm as Princess Poison slipped her hand into her pocket and produced Princess Ella's wand. "Princess Poison's going to do some magic!"

Princess Poison whispered a spell and flicked the wand.

Charlotte gripped Mia's arm. "What has she done now?"

"I don't know," Mia said anxiously.

Just then, there was a clatter in the ring and the crowd groaned. Mia looked round and saw that Peanut had just knocked one of the jumps down. Grace would get a penalty point. Mia's eyes widened. "Charlotte! The jumps!"

All the jumps had suddenly got much bigger! Grace was looking confused as she and Peanut headed towards the next jump.

"Princess Poison must have cast a spell!" said Charlotte.

"Those jumps are too high," said Mia in alarm. "Why hasn't anyone noticed?"

"Because of Princess Poison's magic, of course!" Charlotte said. She turned to glare furiously at Princess Poison, who wiggled her fingers in a mocking wave.

Mia watched, heart in mouth, as Peanut approached a big, red jump. It looked enormous. Peanut hesitated as he came up to it but then bravely tried to run faster.

"No!" Charlotte gasped. The jump was much too high for Peanut to clear safely. Grace pulled him away from it and they rode around it instead.

"Oh dear," Mia said. "That's Peanut's second penalty."

"We've got to do something, Mia!" Charlotte said, pulling out her necklace.

"If Grace gets any more penalties she won't have a chance of winning the competition. And if Princess Poison spoils her wish, Princess Ella will be banished from Wishing Star Palace. We have to think of something!"

CHAPTER SIX

Cross-Country Challenge

Charlotte and Mia fitted their pendants together. "I wish the jumps would go back to the right height!" whispered Charlotte.

There was a flash of light. All the jumps were at the correct height again.

Princess Poison shrieked in anger.

Grace cantered back towards the red jump and this time, Peanut leapt over it cleanly.

He finished the rest of the course perfectly, clearing every fence.

"So, just a couple of unfortunate errors for Grace Purcell riding Peanut!" said the announcer. "Grace slips to fourth position on the leader board. But that could all change in the cross-country round. There's still everything to ride for!"

The crowd clapped as Grace rode out, patting Peanut.

Charlotte and Mia ran to meet her.

"Did you see that?" she said to them. "The jumps suddenly got enormous."

"It was Princess Poison. She cast a spell," said Mia. "We had to use another wish to get the jumps back to normal."

"Thanks," said Grace. "Oh, I wish I hadn't missed those jumps. But if Peanut and I do well in the cross-country round there's still a chance we might win."

"Only if we stop Princess Poison from doing something mean again," Mia whispered to Charlotte as they followed Grace to the trailer.

Grace changed her jacket for a long-sleeved red and blue top. Then the girls helped her brush out Peanut's mane, so Grace could hang on to it when going over the big cross-country fences.

As they worked, she told them how the cross-country was judged. "There are jumps and ditches spread out over several fields.

You have to go over them in the right order and finish within the time limit or you get penalty points. You also get a penalty point if your horse doesn't go over one of the jumps."

"How do you know where to go?" said Charlotte.

"There are flags to guide you. You must jump with the red flag on your right and the white flag on your left or you get eliminated." She patted Peanut. "This is it, boy. You've got to do well!"

When they got to the start of the cross-country course, there were lots of spectators gathered round.

"Most people watch from here, but you

can also watch from one of the fields. You have plenty of time, because I'm the last rider," Grace told them. "Just stay behind the rope barriers and look out for horses galloping past."

"I can think of something more dangerous than galloping horses that we need to look out for," Charlotte muttered to Mia as they set off to find a place to watch from. "And that's Princess Poison!"

Taking care to stay behind the safety ropes, they headed towards a small hill. From the top they had a good view of the jumps spread out in the surrounding fields. White and red flags waved in the breeze, marking out the course.

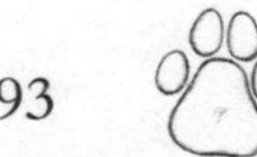

Charlotte and Mia watched as the horses galloped round the course. There were judges dotted all around, taking notes.

"It's nearly time for Grace to start," said Mia. "We should be able to see her coming over the first jumps in a moment."

"What's that horse doing?" said Charlotte as a big black horse came galloping across the field towards them.

"It's heading over here!" said Mia in surprise. She shielded her eyes from the sun and as she did so she saw that the horse's rider was a tall, skinny woman dressed in green leggings and a green top. "Charlotte, look! It's Princess Poison!" she gasped in horror.

Princess Poison reached the girls and reined in her horse. Its eyes were glowing with a fierce green light.

She pulled Princess Ella's wand from her pocket, pointed it at a jump in the distance and called out a spell:

**"Magic, make the field
all boggy,
Turn the grass muddy
and soggy!"**

The field instantly turned to swampy marshland.

"Now let's see how your friend's pony does in that soggy field," said Princess Poison. "Good luck – or as I like to say, break a leg!" Cackling, she cried, "Giddy-up, Striker!" and galloped past them.

Charlotte and Mia gazed at the field in horror. The jump wasn't safe any more – Peanut could get hurt when he landed!

"Grace and Peanut are coming!" cried Charlotte.

She pointed to where the chestnut pony was racing towards the muddy jump. Grace clung on for dear life. As Peanut got closer to the jump, his hooves seemed to get sucked down into the mud. Struggling, he leaped up, soaring into the air.

"Quick!" gasped Mia, pulling out her necklace. "We have to do something before he lands!" The pendants were shining dimly now because they just had one wish left.

They put the half hearts together. "I wish the course was dry and safe," said Mia.

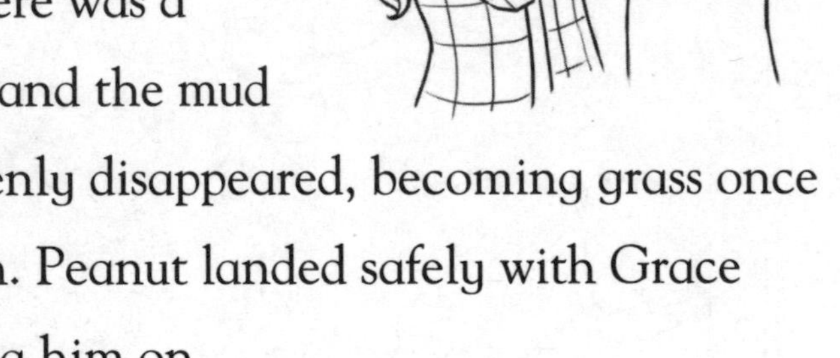

There was a flash and the mud suddenly disappeared, becoming grass once again. Peanut landed safely with Grace urging him on.

"Phew! We did it!" Charlotte said, sighing with relief.

They cheered as Grace and Peanut started to leap over the rest of the jumps perfectly.

There was a harsh cawing overhead.

Charlotte frowned. "What's that noise?"

Looking up, they saw a green parrot flying out of the trees. It swooped through the air towards the last jump. "Ha ha ha!" it cawed. "Venom want a flag!"

"It's Princess Poison's parrot, Venom!" said Mia. "What's he doing?"

The parrot swooped down and grabbed one of the flags by the water jump.

He tossed it to the ground. Then he flapped to another and did the same thing.

"Why is he moving the flags?" asked Charlotte.

Venom flapped off, shrieking triumphantly.

The judge nearest to the jump was writing in his notebook and didn't seem to have noticed what the parrot had done.

"If Grace doesn't jump in the right place she'll be eliminated!" Mia cried. "We've got to do something!"

"But we've used up all our wishes!" Charlotte said in dismay. "There's no more magic left!"

CHAPTER SEVEN

A Wish is Granted!

"We can solve this without magic," Mia said. "But we'll have to be quick. Come on!"

They ducked under the rope safety barrier and raced across the grass towards the water jump. Could they get there in time?

The judge called out, "Hey! What are you girls doing?"

But there was no time to explain.

Charlotte glanced round and saw Peanut galloping towards them. "Hurry!" she panted.

Mia and Charlotte each grabbed a flag from the ground. Luckily, they'd watched the other horses jumping so they both knew where they went. They jammed the flags back in place and jumped out of the way just as Grace came galloping up.

She looked surprised to see them but urged Peanut on. "Come on, boy. You can do it!" He bravely leapt over the fence into the water, splashed through, and got out at exactly the right point.

Charlotte punched the air and whooped. "They did it!"

Grace looked over her shoulder and grinned, then urged Peanut on to the finish. He galloped across the grass, heading towards the spectators.

"They didn't get any penalties at all!" Mia gasped, hugging Charlotte excitedly.

"I think they might win!"

She and Charlotte ran across the field towards the finish. When they got there, they heard an announcement over the sound system. "And first prize goes to … Grace Purcell, riding Peanut!"

Grace threw her arms around Peanut's neck and buried her face in his mane. Then she dismounted and hugged her parents. She was mud-spattered but had a huge grin on her face.

"Peanut did it!" Grace cried as Mia and Charlotte ran up to her. "He won!"

"You did absolutely brilliantly, darling," her mum said.

"It wasn't me. It was Peanut," said Grace, her eyes shining.

Her mum smiled. "Peanut does seem to look after you."

"He really does," said Grace. "I know he doesn't have a lot of experience, but he's very talented."

"If he's this good now, he'll be even better when he's a bit older," said her dad, thoughtfully. Then he gave a big grin. "All right, Grace. If you still want him, he's yours."

"Oh, I do want him. I want him so much!" gasped Grace, hugging Peanut again. He nuzzled her and whinnied happily. Suddenly a double rainbow appeared in the sky. The two perfect arches shimmered and shone. As everyone noticed and pointed, happiness exploded through Mia. Grace's wish had come true!

"Thank you for your help! Thank you so much!" Grace said to the girls.

"We loved helping you and Peanut," said Mia, giving her a hug.

"Have fun with him," said Charlotte. They both gave Peanut a pat, hugged Grace goodbye and then left her to celebrate with her mum and dad.

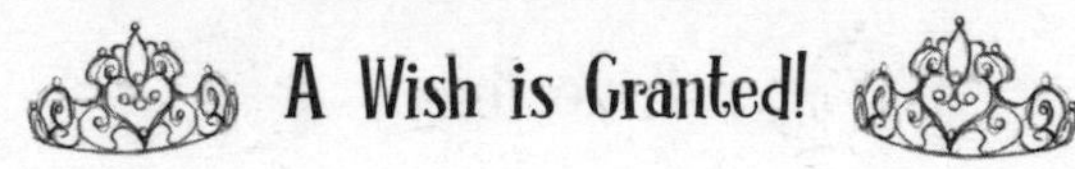

"GAH!" Looking round, they saw Princess Poison standing beside her horse, Striker. Venom was perched on her shoulder. Hex was struggling to hold on to Crusher as he pulled on his lead.

"You brats!" Princess Poison hissed at them. "You did it again! You ruined all my plans!"

"Oh yes, I guess we did," Charlotte said with a grin.

"And we'll *keep* ruining them," said Mia. "We won't let you make people unhappy."

"Next time, I'll beat you, just see if I don't," hissed Princess Poison. "Come, Hex!" She tugged her horse's reins, pulling it round.

Mia gasped and pointed. The saddlebag on Princess Poison's horse was open and the tip of Princess Ella's wand was sticking out of it. Charlotte leapt forward to grab it.

"SQUAWK!" shrieked Venom.

Princess Poison swung round with a snarl that could have matched Crusher's. "Oh no, you don't!" she said, whipping the wand out of the saddlebag and holding it up high. "Your princess friend is never getting this wand back. Never!" She brandished it in the air.

But as she did so, she accidentally hit Striker on the nose with the wand. He reared up. Princess Poison staggered and lost her balance. *SPLAT!* She fell on her bottom, right in a pile of horse manure.

"Argh!" she shrieked in fury.

"Are you all right, mistress?" fussed Hex, but as he came over to try and help, Miss Fluffy and Crusher both dived into the manure pile in delight, sending the stinky stuff flying all over Princess Poison's clothes and hair.

Princess Poison spoke through gritted teeth. "Get. Me. Out. Of. Here."

She waved the wand and in a green flash they all vanished. Charlotte and Mia burst out laughing.

"Girls!" They turned and saw Alice coming towards them in riding clothes. She was smiling broadly. "I've been watching in the Magic Mirror. You've done amazingly well. Grace is thrilled that her wish has been granted. Well done!" She hugged them. "Now it's time you had your reward." She pulled out her wand and touched it to their pendants.

In a flash of light, a new ruby appeared in each half heart. "You're one step closer to passing your next stage of training and getting your princess slippers," Alice said.

"I just wish we could have got Princess Ella's wand back for her," said Charlotte.

"Maybe next time," said Alice kindly.

"Ella's just pleased you helped Grace and stopped Princess Poison from spoiling her wish – that's the most important thing. Oh, and she also wanted to know if you've thought of any names for the baby dragons yet."

"Not yet," said Charlotte.

Mia glanced over to where Grace was stroking Peanut and talking happily to her mum and dad. "I've got an idea," she said suddenly. "How about Grace and Peanut? The girl dragon could be Grace – she's so pretty and graceful."

"Oh yes!" gasped Charlotte. "And the boy dragon is so little and cute that Peanut would be the perfect name for him!"

Alice smiled. "Grace and Peanut it is! I'll tell Ella. But for now, it's time for you to say goodbye and go back to your homes."

The girls hugged. "See you very soon, I hope," Charlotte told Mia.

"For another adventure!" Mia agreed.

Alice waved her wand and the girls were swept away in glittering whirlwinds of light.

Mia landed in her living room. She shook her head and blinked. It was amazing to think she'd been at a horse show just moments ago! Flossie was rolling round on the carpet with her new toy and Mia could hear Gran humming to herself in the kitchen as she made their drinks.

"Oh, Flossie," said Mia, crouching down and stroking her cat. "I've had such an incredible time."

Flossie purred.

The door opened and Gran came in with the drinks. "Flossie loves her toy!" she said.

"What are you going to make next?"

Mia sipped her hot chocolate thoughtfully. "I think I'd like to make another toy for Flossie," she said. "A pink dragon!"

Gran raised her eyebrows. "I didn't know dragons could be pink."

Mia grinned. If only Gran knew! "Oh yes, Gran," she said confidently. "They definitely can!"

The End

Join Charlotte and Mia in their next Secret Princesses adventure

Read on for a sneak peek!

Kitten Wish

Charlotte Williams blew her curly brown hair out of her eyes and tightened her grip on the bat. This was it. There were only two minutes left. If she scored a run, her team would win!

She could hear her team-mates calling out and she knew her family would be cheering her from the stands. The pitcher threw the ball. Charlotte swung the bat but missed.

"Strike!" the umpire called.

Charlotte bit her lip. She didn't want to miss again.

The pitcher threw again and the ball came hurtling towards Charlotte.

Thwack! She sent the ball flying through the air. Yes! She sprinted round the bases. First base. Second base …

"Go, Charlotte! Go, Charlotte!" her team-mates shrieked.

From the corner of her eye, Charlotte spotted a player throwing the ball. She ran as fast as she could – and slid into home base just before the catcher caught the ball in her glove.

She'd done it! The umpire blew a blast on the whistle to finish the game. Her team had won by one run!

Charlotte's team-mates raced over.

"That was awesome!" gasped Leah, one of Charlotte's new friends.

Coach Jacobson high-fived her. "Great work, Charlotte!" he said. "It sure is hard to believe you didn't play softball until this season."

"Didn't you play when you lived in England?" Leah asked curiously.

"Nope," said Charlotte. "In England I played rounders and netball."

"Do you miss playing those games?" Leah asked.

Charlotte shook her head. "One of the best things about moving to California has been trying lots of new sports!" She grinned. "And the sunshine, of course!"

Coach Jacobson clapped his hands. "Time to get changed, ladies."

The team headed to the locker room. Charlotte's mind was buzzing. Her softball top was dirty, but the game had been so much fun. She couldn't wait to tell Mia about it.

Mia was her best friend. She was back in England, and leaving her had been the hardest thing about moving to California. Luckily, the two friends had discovered they could still see each other in an amazing way – using magic!

Before Charlotte had left for California, their old babysitter, Alice, had given them matching necklaces. Every so often, the necklaces would start to glow and then Charlotte and Mia would be whisked away to a secret place high in the clouds called Wishing Star Palace. It was so amazing! Alice had explained that they had been selected to train as Secret Princesses – very special girls who could magically help people by granting wishes.

Charlotte reached the locker room and took her clothes into a cubicle to get changed. As she changed her softball top for a lilac T-shirt she touched her golden necklace with its half-heart shaped pendant.

Oh, I hope Mia and I get to meet up again soon, she thought longingly. Just then, her pendant started to glow. Charlotte squealed and then clapped a hand over her mouth, hoping no one had heard. The magic was working again!

She clutched the pendant. "I wish I could see Mia!" she whispered.

Light swirled out of the necklace and Charlotte felt herself being whisked away. She spun round and round in a tunnel of light and landed on soft grass. Opening her eyes, she saw flowerbeds overflowing with gorgeous lilac and pink blooms, a velvet-soft lawn and trees hung with fluffy candyfloss and rainbow-swirled lollipops. The gorgeous golden turrets of Wishing Star Palace towered in the distance.

It was so good to be back at Wishing Star Palace! Her clothes had magically transformed into her beautiful pink princess dress and strappy silver sandals. Charlotte spun around, the full skirt twirling around her legs.

Read Kitten Wish to find out what happens next!

Princess Ella's Pony Care Tips

Ponies are gorgeous animals – and best of all you can ride them! If you are lucky enough to have your own pony, follow Princess Ella's advice for keeping it healthy and happy.

- Always make sure your pony has plenty of clean water to drink. Keep its water trough clean and check that the water isn't frozen in winter.

- Feed your pony good quality hay and a small amount of grain, depending on its size, age and how much exercise it gets.

- Keep your pony in a fenced pasture so it cannot escape and it is safe from dogs and predators. Make sure your pony has shelter from sun, rain and wind, and dry ground to stand on.

- Horses are social animals and enjoy having company. Let your pony spend as much time as possible pastured with other horses.

Equipment List:

- Water trough
- Feed tub
- Hay net
- Halter
- Lead rope
- Bedding
- Grooming kit
- First aid kit

Dos and Don'ts

DO let your pony graze and run in the pasture as much as possible.

DON'T feed your pony right before or after exercise as it will give it an upset tummy.

DO make sure that your pony's tack fits properly as poorly fitting equipment can cause pain.

DON'T shout at or punish your pony. Reward good behaviour with praise and treats.

♥ FREE NECKLACE ♥

In every book of Secret Princesses series two: The Ruby Collection, there is a special Wish Token. Collect all four tokens to get an exclusive Best Friends necklace for you and your best friend!

Simply fill in the form below, send it in with your four tokens and we'll send you your special necklaces.*

Send to: Secret Princesses Wish Token Offer, Hachette Children's Books Marketing Department, Carmelite House, 50 Victoria Embankment, London, EC4Y 0DZ

Closing Date: 31st June 2017

secretprincessesbooks.co.uk

Please complete using capital letters (UK and Republic of Ireland residents only)

FIRST NAME:

SURNAME:

DATE OF BIRTH: DD | MM | YYYY

ADDRESS LINE 1:

ADDRESS LINE 2:

ADDRESS LINE 3:

POSTCODE:

PARENT OR GUARDIAN'S EMAIL ADDRESS:

I'd like to receive regular Secret Princesses email newsletters and information about other great Hachette Children's Group offers (I can unsubscribe at any time).

Terms and Conditions apply. For full terms and conditions please go to secretprincessesbooks.co.uk/terms

1 Secret Princesse Wish Token

BE ST FRIE NDS

*** 2000 necklaces available while stocks Terms and conditions apply.**

♥ WIN A PRINCESS GOODY BAG ♥

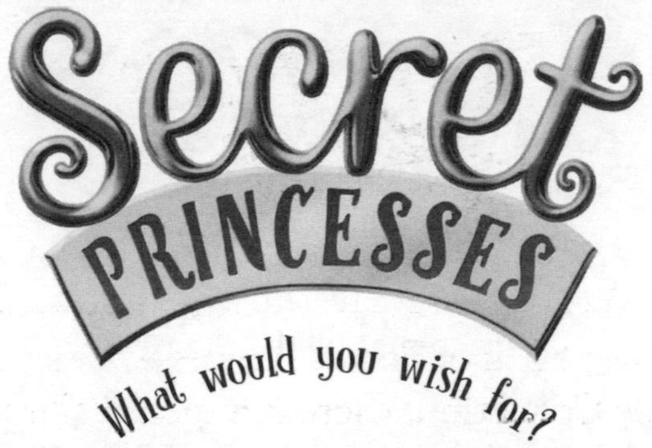

Design your own dress and win a Secret Princesses goody bag for you and your best friend!

Charlotte and Mia get to wear beautiful dresses at Wishing Star Palace, but now they want you to design one for them.

To enter all you have to do is follow these steps:

Go to **www.secretprincessesbooks.co.uk**

- Click the competition module
- Download and print the activity sheet
- Design a beautiful dress for Charlotte or Mia
- Send your entry to:

Secret Princesses: Ruby Collection Competition
Hachette Children's Group
Carmelite House
50 Victoria Embankment
London
EC4Y 0DZ

Closing date: 31st March 2017
For full terms and conditions,
visit www.hachettechildrens.co.uk/terms

Good luck!

What would you wish for?

Are you a Secret Princess?

Join the Secret Princesses Club at:

secretprincessesbooks.co.uk

Explore the magic of the
Secret Princesses and discover:

♥ Special competitions! ♥
♥ Exclusive content! ♥
♥ All the latest princess news! ♥

Open to UK and Republic of Ireland residents only
Please ask your parent/guardian for their permission to join

For full terms and conditions go to
secretprincessesbooks.co.uk/terms

Ruby620

Enter the special code above on the website to receive

50 Princess Points